Just for Today

Jan Phillips

Illustrated by Alison Bonds Shapiro

H J Kramer
Starseed Press
Tiburon, California

Art Director: Linda Kramer

Library of Congress Cataloging-in-Publication Data

Phillips, Jan, 1956–
  Just for today / Jan Phillips ; illustrated by Alison Bonds Shapiro.
       p. cm.
  Summary: The Bear family decides to spend a day ignoring their usual
activities and responsibilities while focusing instead on enjoying each
other's company.
  ISBN 1-932073-07-8 (alk. paper)
  [1. Family life—Fiction. 2. Bears—Fiction. 3. Stories in rhyme.] I.
Shapiro, Alison Bonds, ill. II. Title.
PZ8.3.P5581975Ju 2005
[E]—dc22
                                                              2004008377

H J Kramer
Starseed Press
P.O. Box 1082
Tiburon, California 94920

Printed in Singapore

10 9 8 7 6 5 4 3 2 1

For Ryan, my baby bear.
— J.P.

For Fletcher and Jacob,
the beloved sons who grew up
to be poppa bears.
— A.B.S.

Wake up, sleepy heads!
We have a surprise.
It's just for today,
So open your eyes.

Just for today...
We've planned the day,
To simply be with you.
We'll play with blocks,
Ignore the clocks,
And maybe hide a few.

So just for today...
We'll breakfast on popcorn,
And talk about our wishes.

We'll make some paper airplanes soar
And forget about the dishes.

Just for today...
Let's turn off
The telephone and faxes.
All the world will have to wait,
Including bills and taxes.

So just for today…
We promise not
To yell, or scold, or nag.
We'll laugh at all your silly jokes
And hug you while you brag.

Just for today...
We'll play with you
In any way you say.
We'll finger paint a sky so blue
And flowers bright and gay.

Just for today…
We'll work with clay.
Let's squish it through our fingers.
We'll dress up in our funny hats
And pretend we're opera singers.

So just for today…
Let's ignore the laundry
And run down to the park.

We won't do a blessed thing
But play until it's dark.

Just for today...
We'll toss our shoes
And walk barefoot just for fun.
We'll feel the grass between our toes
And startle everyone.

So just for today…
On our own special day,
We'll spend it all together.
We'll lay on our backs and watch the clouds
And talk about the weather.

Just for today...
We'll all be kids
And juggle jelly beans.
We'll splash in puddles in the park
And fly up on the swings.

Just for today…
We'll play hide-and-seek
And giggle 'til we're found.
We'll ride our bikes until it's night
And we're home safe and sound.

So just for tonight . . .
When we're all tired out,
I'll hold you in my arms.

I'll muss your hair and kiss your cheek
And keep you from all harm.

So just for tonight...
Let's turn the TV off
Then hug each other tight.

We'll count the stars
And say our prayers
And whisper soft goodnights.

So let's give thanks for all we have,
For nothing could be better.
Than knowing there'll be other days
When we will be together.